Under the Sea
Sea Snakes

by Jody Sullivan Rake

Consulting Editor: Gail Saunders-Smith, PhD

Consultant: Debbie Nuzzolo
Education Manager
SeaWorld, San Diego, California

Capstone
press®

Mankato, Minnesota

Pebble Plus is published by Capstone Press,
151 Good Counsel Drive, P.O. Box 669, Mankato, Minnesota 56002.
www.capstonepress.com

1 2 3 4 5 6 12 11 10 09 08 07

Library of Congress Cataloging-in-Publication Data
Rake, Jody Sullivan.
    Sea snakes / by Jody Sullivan Rake.
    p. cm.—(Pebble plus. Under the sea)
    Summary: "Simple text and photographs present the lives of sea snakes"—Provided by publisher.
    Includes bibliographical references (p. 23) and index.
    ISBN-13: 978-0-7368-6725-2 (hardcover)
    ISBN-10: 0-7368-6725-2 (hardcover)
1. Sea snakes—Juvenile literature. I. Title. II. Series: Under the sea (Mankato, Minn.)
QL666.O64R35 2007
597.96'5—dc22   2006013647

Editorial Credits
Mari Schuh, editor; Juliette Peters, set designer; Kim Brown and Patrick D. Dentinger, book designers;
    Wanda Winch, photo researcher/photo editor

Photo Credits
Bruce Coleman Inc./John Visser, 9
Corbis/Stephen Frink, 12–13
Getty Images Inc./The Image Bank/Cousteau Society, 10–11
Marty Snyderman, cover, 19
Minden Pictures/Fred Bavendam, 5
SeaPics.com/Doug Perrine, 1; Jez Tryner, 20–21; Mark Strickland, 16–17; Nigel Marsh, 7, 14–15

Note to Parents and Teachers

The Under the Sea set supports national science standards related to the diversity
and unity of life. This book describes and illustrates sea snakes. The images support
early readers in understanding the text. The repetition of words and phrases helps early
readers learn new words. This book also introduces early readers to subject-specific
vocabulary words, which are defined in the Glossary section. Early readers may need
assistance to read some words and to use the Table of Contents, Glossary, Read More,
Internet Sites, and Index sections of the book.

Table of Contents

What Are Sea Snakes?

Sea snakes

are reptiles that live

in the ocean.

Some sea snakes are
as short as a child's arm.
Others are as long as
a dolphin.

Some sea snakes

leave the ocean.

They crawl on land.

Body Parts

Sea snakes have scales.

They shed their scales

to get rid of bugs.

Flat tails help sea snakes

glide in the ocean.

13

Sea snakes have nostrils
that close under the water.
They open to breathe
above the water.

nostril

What Sea Snakes Do

Sea snakes smell prey
with their forked tongues.

Sea snakes bite prey
with their fangs.
Venom squirts out
and kills the prey.

Under the Sea

Sea snakes live in

warm water

under the sea.

Glossary

fang—a long, sharp tooth; sea snakes have two fangs.

forked—having one end split into two or more parts; sea snakes use their forked tongues to find food.

glide—to move smoothly and easily

nostril—an opening in an animal's nose used for breathing

prey—an animal hunted by another animal for food

reptile—a cold-blooded animal that breathes air and has a backbone; most reptiles have scales.

scale—one of the small, thin plates that cover a reptile

shed—to let something fall off or drop off

venom—poison inside the fangs of some animals

Read More

Klein, Adam G. *Yellow-bellied Sea Snakes.* Checkerboard Animal Library. Edina, Minn.: Abdo, 2006.

Rose, Deborah Lee. *Ocean Babies.* Washington, D.C.: National Geographic Society, 2004.

Rustad, Martha E. H. *Sea Snakes.* Ocean Life. Mankato, Minn.: Capstone Press, 2003.

Internet Sites

FactHound offers a safe, fun way to find Internet sites related to this book. All of the sites on FactHound have been researched by our staff.

Here's how:

1. Visit *www.facthound.com*

2. Choose your grade level.

3. Type in this book ID **0736867252** for age-appropriate sites. You may also browse subjects by clicking on letters, or by clicking on pictures and words.

4. Click on the **Fetch It** button.

FactHound will fetch the best sites for you!

Index

Word Count: 105
Grade: 1
Early-Intervention Level: 12